WHAT COLOR ARE YOU?

by

DARWIN WALTON

**Photographs
Hal Franklin**

An *EBONY JR!* Book

Johnson Publishing Company, Inc., Chicago

TO THE CHILDREN IN MY LIFE
Yesterday was dark.
Blindly it's children wandered seeking understanding.
Children of today,
Use your gifts of sight wisely
And tomorrow will brighter be.

—Darwin McBeth Walton

Library of Congress Catalog Card Number 77-134796
Standard Book Number 87485-045-2
Copyright© 1973 by Johnson Publishing Company, Inc.
Second Printing, 1978
Third Printing, 1985
Printed in the United States of America

WHAT COLOR ARE YOU?

This book is about you. It's about your **basic** needs, your basic feelings, and some of the other things that make you the way you are. It's also about other people who have the same basic needs and basic feelings that you have. It will explain that other people, some of whom may seem quite different from you, do just about the same things you do and for just about the same reasons you do them.

"Basic" means **fundamental** or the things most needed to start with. For example, the need to eat is basic. Everyone must eat in order to live. Different people eat different kinds of food. Some people eat meat, and some don't. Some eat grain, in the form of bread, cereal or rice. Some people eat fish and some even eat insects. Most of us eat **combinations** of different foods, but each of us must certainly eat.

Let's see! Could you think of another of our basic needs? Quickly now! Did you think of sleep? Yes, the need for sleep and rest is basic. Our bodies need rest from activity and a quiet time for growing. Different people sleep in different places and at different times. Some sleep in beds or in **hammocks.** Some people sleep on the floor or on the ground. Some of us sleep during the day while others sleep at night, but each of us must certainly sleep.

Exercise is another basic need. Without exercise, our blood won't circulate well, and our bodies become stiff and unhealthy. People choose different physical activities such as swimming, skiing, playing ball or jumping rope as ways of exercising. Some of us run or walk, but each of us must exercise.

People have the same basic feelings, too. They feel happy or sad, lonesome or loved. Of course, people have different **reactions** to **experiences** that they share—there are both winners and losers in a ball game—but they do **react.**

As surely as food, rest, and exercise are necessary for a healthy body, so love, **appreciation,** and **self-respect** are necessary for a **healthy,** happy mind.

In order that we may **satisfy** our basic
needs and feelings, each **human being** is born with
five **senses.** Think for a moment, and try to name
them.

Sight, hearing, smell, taste and touch are the
five senses you should have named.

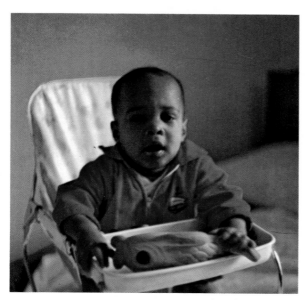

Photo by A. C. Vivian

These are the tools we use to discover the world around us. Even though each person uses his senses to learn about his **particular surroundings,** different people react in different ways. For **example,** you may love the taste of strawberry ice cream, but someone else in your family may not like it at all.

You can probably think of many other ways in which people react differently to the same sights, sounds, odors, flavors, and feelings.

9

All over the world, people have the same **general appearance.** We all walk in an **upright position** on two legs and feet. We all have the same **vital organs** such as heart, liver, lungs, stomach, and skin, which perform the same basic **functions.**

We all have **similar** body **structures** for making use of our tools—the five senses. We have eyes for seeing, ears for hearing, noses for smelling, mouths and tongues for tasting, hands for touching and holding, and skin for feeling heat and pain. Our body structure and senses help us to meet our basic needs and feelings, and they help us to **adapt** to our **surroundings.**

Although people are **basically** the same,
each person is a **distinctly** different **individual.**
Each of us has a **particular** way of doing things.
For example, each person walks in a special way;
each person talks and laughs in a special way.
We are all a little different from anyone else in size
and shape. One of the **differences** in people
we notice easily is the **variation** of skin coloring.

Have you ever wondered why?

Photo by A. C. Vivian

The reason can be explained quite simply.
Light allows us to see differences in color.
As tiny babies, we learn quickly to tell light from
darkness. Babies like to play with colorful toys
before they even talk or walk. Color becomes
important in our early learning **processes.**

As we grow older, we often think first of
color when **describing** or **identifying** things we see
every day. So it's **perfectly natural** for us to notice
how people differ in color.

    As you learn more about skin color, you may
want to find out why **society,** or people as a
whole, are sometimes **affected** by your skin color.
You may wonder why the color of another
person's skin can be important to you. There will
probably be other questions that you will want
to ask. So let's find out what causes the
different shades and colors of our skin.

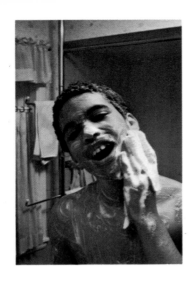

Our skin is made up of two main layers. These layers of **cells** protect and service our bodies in several ways. One of the **protections provided** by our skin helps us to understand why there are different skin colors. Found among the layers of our skin are tiny grains of coloring matter called **pigment.** There are several different pigments, but the one most **responsible** for skin color is a dark **substance** called **melanin.**

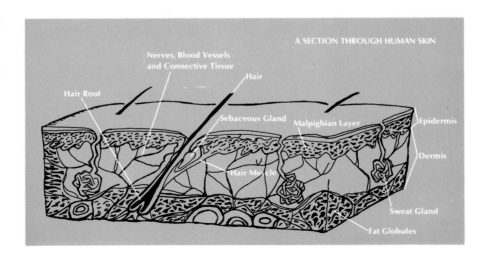

A SECTION THROUGH HUMAN SKIN

Nerves, Blood Vessels and Connective Tissue

Hair

Hair Root

Sebaceous Gland

Malpighian Layer

Epidermis

Dermis

Hair Muscle

Sweat Gland

Fat Globules

Melanin **protects** our skin from the sometimes harmful rays of the sun. Each of us has melanin in our skin. If we are light-skinned, our melanin supply differs from dark-skinned people only in the way it is **scattered** throughout our skin layers and in the amount that is scattered.

The amount of melanin we have in our skin depends upon where our forefathers lived for thousands of years. If our **forefathers** lived near the **equator,** where the sun's rays are most direct, we probably have large amounts of melanin in our skin. This has happened because our skin reacts to the sun's rays and makes an extra amount of melanin when it is needed. Our forefathers who lived near the equator needed this extra protection.

If our forefathers lived in cold northern lands for thousands of years, there was no need for them to develop this extra amount of melanin in their skin.

No matter what color we are, our skin darkens when **exposed** to the sun. This fact has helped **scientists** prove that protection is the basic reason for the color differences in man's skin.

How can it be explained?

Have you ever had a painful **sunburn?** Did you wonder why it happened? This can happen if you don't wait for your body to make enough melanin to protect the **nerve endings** and **blood vessels** in your skin. You can safely build up enough melanin in your skin by getting a little sun at a time. Dark-skinned people have better **protection** against sunburn than light-skinned people, but everyone can be burned by the sun.

Could you explain why?

The darker your **suntan** gets—the longer you can stay in the sun without burning. When summer is over and you are no longer playing out in the sunshine, your skin loses its tan and lightens to its natural color. Suppose you lived in a place where it's sunny and warm all year long. You would have a suntan for protection as long as you played in the sun. A suntanned skin can be light tan or almost black depending on what color your skin is naturally.

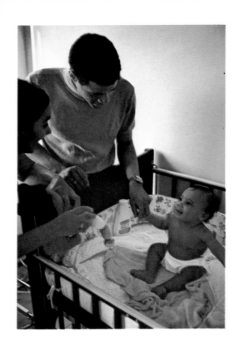

Why are our skin shades different? Why are there different shades of color even in members of the same family?

If one **parent** is dark-skinned and the other parent is light-skinned, the color of their children's skin may be light, dark, or any shade found between the two. Can you understand how this could happen? The children's color would depend upon the amounts of melanin **inherited** from one or both parents.

Sometimes a child is darker or lighter than either of his parents. The amount and placement of inherited melanin cells could explain such a happening.

How did it all begin?

Thousands of years ago, it was difficult and dangerous to move from one place to another. Therefore, groups of people stayed in the one part of the world where they had first settled for many **generations.** Through a process of change called **genetic mutation** or **alteration of generations,** each group developed special **physical** or **racial traits** and skin shades. This enabled them to adapt to their **environment.**

People living near the equator needed more protection from the sun than those in colder **climates.** The bodies of those settled near the equator formed the **habit** of making more melanin. Their skins remained dark as they passed this protection on from generation to generation.

As people **advanced** in **skills** and **knowledge,** they were able to move about more freely. They **migrated** from place to place and the **"races"** became mixed. This resulted in many different shades of skin color.

In the beginning, all man was of one color; today we see different shades of this one color.

Today we see people with skins of all shades from pale **pinkish-beige** to the deepest of brownish-black. Nobody has truly black or truly white skin.

Look at the white of this page. That's a true white! Look at the black print of the letters found on this page. That's a true black! You have never seen anyone with skin that is a true white or black. Our **circulating** blood gives the whitest and the blackest of skins a certain rosy glow.

Look around at the eyes of the persons nearest you now. You may see eyes of blue or gray, green, hazel, brown or nearly black shades.

Which eye color do you think has the most pigment?

Which eye color has the least, or smallest amount of pigment?

Shades of hair color range from black to white with shades of reds, golds, browns, and grays in between. Look around again. You'll find all **combinations** of eye, hair, and skin shades.

What do you think has happened when a person has freckles?

Color, and the many shades of each color, help make life more interesting and enjoyable. Color makes the **identification** of people and things easier. Wouldn't it be dull if all the flowers were the same shade of purple or all the houses were painted the same shade of yellow, or weren't painted at all?

Try **imagining** all the people you know having the same color of eyes, hair and skin. That wouldn't be at all **exciting.** When you meet a new friend, it's much easier to **describe** him in terms of skin, hair and eye color. It wouldn't be quite so easy to speak of him only in terms of his size and shape.

Try describing your best friend or your favorite outfit without using a color to help you.

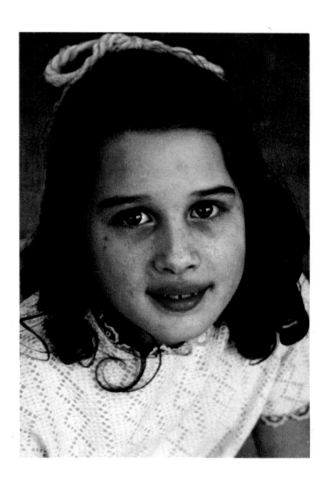

We have seen that skin color and its many variations came about mostly through the need for protection from the sun. We can say that color differences allow us to identify each other and other objects more easily. Now we are going to see just how color adds **variety** and beauty to our lives.

WHO ARE YOU?

Are you Debbie, Anthony, Johnny or James, Willie, Chip or Sue?

Are you Michael, Karen, Cheryl, Jean, Ingrid or LaRue?

No matter what your name may be, it would only be **confusing** if everybody looked the same.

That wouldn't be amusing.

It's great that Bobbie is not like Sam, and Bev is not like Sue. You know they're glad to be themselves just as you're glad

YOU

ARE

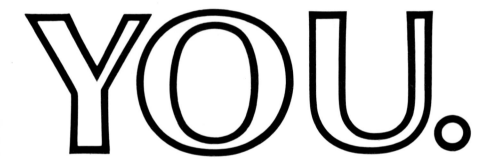

WHAT IS COLOR?

Is it just the way we see things or is it something
more? What does it make us feel?
Let's read, think and explore.

Then, let's think some more.

CAN COLOR BE TASTED?

Can you tell a color from its taste? No peeking now. Does red taste of strawberry, cherry or cinnamon? Does yellow taste vanilla, banana or lemon? There are red mints and green mints and white mints and blue mints! There's chocolate— light and dark.

CAN COLOR BE SMELLED?

What pretty roses! One is red and one is yellow. How can I choose? The **fragrance** is the same.

CAN COLOR BE HEARD?

If you hear a bird sing, can you guess his color? Probably not!

CAN COLOR BE TOUCHED OR FELT?

Beautiful butterfly, you seem a happy fellow. Do you know your **companion's** color?

When you touch the hand of a friend can you feel its blackness or whiteness?

What is the purpose of a person's skin?

It protects the **glands, nerve endings** and **tissues** of the body. That is its purpose.

Does color matter?

Can you guess the color of this person's skin?

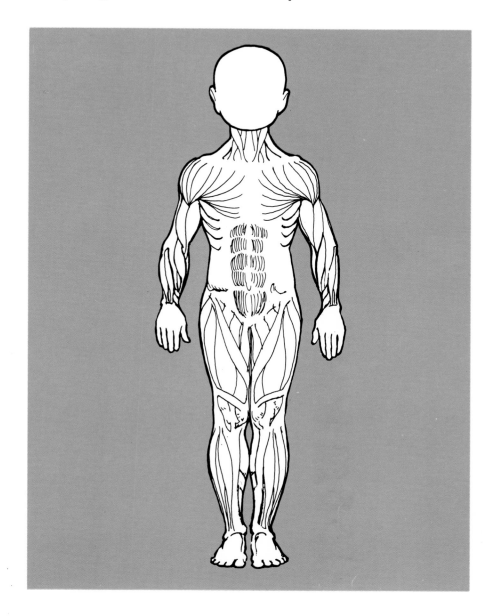

Does color change its **usefulness** or the **organs** it protects?

Does color have anything to do with the way a family feels? Does color change the way a brother feels for a sister?

Photo by A. C. Vivian

Playing games is always fun. We all need exercise. Almost any activity helps keep you well. Having fun is nice no matter what your color.

Have you ever made a new friend on a plane, train, bus or at camp? Have you ever found a friend with whom you shared something special? Have you ever found a friend you learned to trust? It can happen to you!

Love and friendship are color-blind.

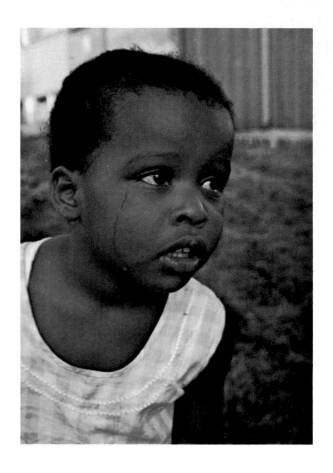

Sometimes there are tears to shed. Some pains come from the outside. Did you ever fall and skin your knee? Can you always keep the tears inside? That is an easy kind of pain to explain. But there are tears we cannot show and pain we cannot talk about. It happens to all of us.

Do you think somebody is lonely today? Do you think there may be someone who has no friend? Could you help to bring happy colors into his life?

Can color be felt if you make someone unhappy because his skin coloring may be lighter or darker than yours?

Does this ever happen in our society?

Have you ever been hungry? For real? Do you know how empty hunger can make you feel?

Can life be colorful and good if you are hungry and hurting inside for food?

Photo by UNICEF

Whatever the shade of your skin may be, hunger has no color that you can see.

Wouldn't it feel good to share a treat with a hungry boy or girl somewhere?

Would you care about the color of his skin?

47

When you're a member of a team, what shades do winning and losing mean? What about the fun that follows the game?

Should the color be the same?

Are you a **curious** person? Do you enjoy learning about people, places and things that may seem strange and different? Your **curiosity** just may prove that they may be quite like many people, places and things you already know.

How about being **creative?** Does your color make a difference? Does your color mean you can do a job well? Everyone has something to **contribute.**

Think of the beauty and variety that color brings into our lives. It plays such an important part in each of our lives.

Whatever shade your skin may be, it protects your body no matter what your color, your shade or your name. It lets you be you and only you.

Whether you're Betty, William, Tanya, Heide, Claudette, Timothy or Larry, the same thing is true.

WHAT COLOR ARE YOU?

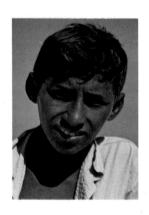

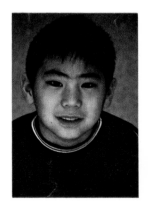

GLOSSARY These pages will help you to say some of the words in WHAT COLOR ARE YOU? It will also help you to understand the meanings of the words as they are used in the book. Use the key below to help you sound the words. You may use a dictionary to discover if any of the words have other meanings.

Pronunciation Key

ă	fat	ĕ	men	ĭ	it
ā	cake	ē	me	ī	ride
â	car	êr	her	îr	bird
ã	care	ẽr	ear		
aw	saw				
ä	father				

ŏ	not	ŭ	us	ōō	moon
ō	old	ū	use	ŏŏ	foot
ô	horse	ûr	burn	oi	oil
ö	soft			ou	out

If the vowels in a word have one of these marks: ȧ ė i ȯ u̇—that will mean that the letter makes an unaccented sound.

Glossary

The root words are defined whenever word endings have been added.

A

Page 10 **adapt** (ȧ dăpt') To adjust, to make fit or suitable.

Page 24 **advance** (ȧd văns') improvement.
advances

Page 22 **alteration of generations** (ȯl tĕ rā'shŭn) (jĕn ė rā'shŭns) body cell changes that have taken place in the bodies of one's forefathers.

Page 33   **amuse** (á mūz′) to entertain in a playful way. **amusing**

Page 7   **appreciation** (á prē shĭ ā′shėn) to think highly of.

B

Page 11   **basic** (bā′sĭk) forming the bottom, fundamental. **basically**

Page 18   **blood vessel** (blŏod, blūd) (vĕs′ĕl) any tube in which blood circulates, an artery, a vein, or a capillary.

C

Page 14   **cell** (sĕl) a tiny mass that is the fundamental unit of living matter.

Page 6, 25   **circulate** (sêr′kū lāt) to pass from one place to another. **circulating**

Page 23   **climate** (klĭ′mĭt) the average weather conditions at a place over a period of years.

Page 4   **combination** (kŏm bĭ nā′shĭn) two or more things together.

Page 39   **companion** (kŭm păn′yŭn) a friend or an associate.

Page 33   **confuse** (kŭn fūz′) to mix up. **confusing**

Page 51   **contribute** (kŭn trĭb′ūt) to give along with others.

Page 51   **creative** (krē ā′tĭv) inventive, productive.

Page 50   **curious** (kū′rĭ ŭs) wanting to learn or know. **curiosity** (kū rĭ ŏs′i tē)

D

Page 12   **describe** (dĕ skrīb′) to give an account of in words.
describing

Page 11   **distinct** (dĭs tīnkt′) different from others.
distinctly (dĭs tīngkt′)

E

Page 22   **environment** (ĕn vī′rŭn mėnt) surroundings; the conditions that affect the growth and development of a person, an animal or a plant.

Page 16   **equator** (ē kwā′têr) an imaginary circle around the earth, halfway between the North Pole and the South Pole.

Page 9   **example** (ĕks ăm′pėl) a model or a sample.

Page 6   **exercise** (ĕks′êr sīz) a regular series of movements to strengthen some part of the body.
exercising

Page 7   **experience** (ĕks pēr′ĭ ėns) observation or practice resulting in more knowledge.

Page 17   **expose** (ĕks pōz′) not having shelter.
exposed

F

Page 16   **forefather** (fôr′fäth êr) a relative or ancestor from a much earlier time.

Page 37   **fragrant** (frā′grănt) sweet in smell.
fragrance

Page 27   **freckle** (frĕk′ėl) a small, brown spot on the skin.

Page 10   **function** (fŭngk′shĭn) work, use, or purpose.

Page 4   **fundamental** (fŭn dė mĕn′tėl) basic; at the very bottom or beginning.
fundamentally

G

H

I

K

M

Page 14   **melanin** (mĕl′ȧ nĭn) the black pigment of the skin, eyes, hair, and other animal tissue.

Page 24   **migrate** (mī′grāt) to move from one country or region to another.
migrated

N

Page 12   **natural** (năch′ė rėl) expected or accepted.

Page 18   **nerve ending** (nêrv) (ĕnd′ĭng) the end of a cell which lets you feel warmth, chill, pain and other sensations.

O

Page 41   **organ** (ôr′gĭn) any part of the body that performs some special job.

P

Page 21   **parent** (pãr′ėnt) father or mother.

Page 11   **particular** (pâr tĭk′ū lėr) separate and distinct, special.

Page 6   **physical activity** (fĭz′ĭ kėl) (ac tĭv′ĭ tē) body movement or exercise.

Page 14   **pigment** (pĭg′mėnt) coloring matter; a pigment cell produces or makes coloring in animals and plants.

Page 25   **pinkish-beige** (pĭngk′ĭsh) (bāzh) a combination of pale-red and pale-tan.

Page 12   **process** (prŏs′ĕs) a series of actions moving toward a certain end.
processes

Page 14 **protect** (prō tĕkt′) to guard against harm or danger.
protection

Page 14 **provide** (prō vīd′) to supply what is needed.
provided

R

Page 24 **race** (rās) a tribe, a people, or a nation who have been able to breed and live together for long periods of time.
races

Page 22 **racial** (rā′shel) having to do with race.

Page 7 **react** (rē ăkt′) to be affected, to think or act in a certain way.
reaction

Page 14 **responsible** (rĭ spön′sĭ bĭl) to have as a duty.

S

Page 8 **satisfy** (săt′ĭs fĭ) happy or contented.

Page 15 **scatter** (skăt′têr) found here and there.
scattered

Page 17 **scientist** (sī′ĕn tĭst) person who works in science.

Page 7 **self-respect** (sĕlf) (rē spĕkt′) to think well of oneself and to cause others to think well of you.

Page 8 **sense** (sĕns) the way the body uses one of the organs provided for seeing, smelling, tasting, hearing and touching.
senses

Page 24 **skill** (skĭl) able to perform crafts; to be able to use inventions, science.
skills

Page 13 **society** (sō sī′e tǐ) all people; any group of people joined together because- of some common interest.

Page 10 **structure** (strŭk′chêr) the way something is put together or built.
structures

Page 14 **substance** (sŭb′stėns) what a thing is made of.

Page 18 **sunburn** (sŭn′bêrn) a red and painful condition of the skin caused by too much sun.

Page 19 **suntan** (sŭn′tăn) when the skin darkens because of being in the sun.
suntanned

Page 10 **surround** (sêr round′) living conditions that are around one.
surroundings

T

Page 40 **tissue** (tǐsh′ū) a layer of cells in the human body.
tissues

Page 22 **trait** (trāt) features or characteristics that set something or someone apart from others.

U

Page 10 **upright position** (ŭp′rǐt) (pō zǐsh ėn) to be erect or standing upwards.

V

Page 11 **variation** (vãr ǐ ā′shŭn) a change, somewhat different.

Page 30 **variety** (vȧ rǐ′ė tǐ) a mixture of different things.

Page 10 **vital** (vī′tėl) very necessary for life.

61

ABOUT THE AUTHOR

Ms. Darwin Walton, a teacher in the DuPage County (Illinois) School District #3, has written a warm and reasonable response to the question so often asked by her students, *"What Color Am I?"*

What Color Are You? does not engage in special pleading, but does explain the role of color in our lives and the scientific basis of skin color. Ms. Walton's faith in the innate intelligence, wit and wisdom of children is unlimited and her ability to communicate with them is evident. She has also been a teacher in the Chicago Public Schools where she taught students in the inner-city and she has been a Curriculum Coordinator and Teacher Supervisor in the Maywood (Ill.) Headstart Program.

ABOUT THE PHOTOGRAPHER

Hal Franklin, a New York photographer, whose work has been seen in Ebony, Black Stars and Jet Magazines is now studying medicine.

ACKNOWLEDGEMENTS

With few exceptions, the American children in this book are children in my life. Many I have known since birth. The situations depicted here are real and the photographs were taken under natural circumstances. To these children and their parents or guardians I express my thanks and appreciation. I am also indebted to Miss N. Poulouskie at UNICEF, for permission to use photographs as credited.

The prospectus for this book was developed in a course of study under the direction of Mrs. Dorothy Koller, Coordinator of Teacher Training for DuPage County. It was her suggestion that I attempt to have it published.

Many associate teachers and friends made suggestions and gave encouragement: Mrs. Pat Powill Clark, Music and Art Coordinator for Cornille School; Dr. Keith Hoover, Director for Psychological Services, George Williams College; Mrs. Anna Hasegann; Mrs. Hopely Roberts, editor, York Center Clarion Newspaper; Mrs. Nina Alexander, principal, Churchville Junior High School; and last but most important, my fourth grade class at Cornille School!
—Darwin McBeth Walton